Society Minnesota Historical, Barbara Ann Shadecker Adams

Early Days at Red River Settlement, and Fort Snelling

Reminiscences of Ann Adams, 1821-1829

Society Minnesota Historical, Barbara Ann Shadecker Adams

Early Days at Red River Settlement, and Fort Snelling
Reminiscences of Ann Adams, 1821-1829

ISBN/EAN: 9783744791250

Printed in Europe, USA, Canada, Australia, Japan

Cover: Foto ©Raphael Reischuk / pixelio.de

More available books at **www.hansebooks.com**

EARLY DAYS AT RED RIVER SETTLEMENT,

AND FORT SNELLING.

REMINISCENCES OF MRS. ANN ADAMS.

1821-1829.

PRELIMINARY NOTE.

During the winter of 1886-87, I learned that Mrs. Adams, whose very interesting and valuable reminiscences of a long and eventful life, (a portion of it passed at Fort Snelling) is given below, was visiting one of her grand-children in West St. Paul, and I took advantage of this fact to call upon her, and secure her statement of events and occurrences in early days at Red River and Fort Snelling. The interviews consumed most of two days, and I wrote down, under her dictation, quite a lengthy narrative of her reminiscences of life on our frontier. I found Mrs. Adams to be a lady of much intelligence, with a tenacious memory of the events of seventy years ago, and narrating them with vivid interest, and in the most descriptive and graphic language. Her story is a very entertaining one, and gives valuable data for our early history. In person, Mrs. Adams is a handsome woman, notwithstanding her age, and possessed of a vigorous and elastic physique, which has sustained her during all the hardships of her adventurous career on the frontier, as narrated in the following pages.

J. FLETCHER WILLIAMS.

I cheerfully consent to your request, to give you an account of the hardships and adventures of the party of Swiss emigrants, who, in 1821, went from their native land to Selkirk's Settlement, and many of whom eventually settled in Minnesota; of which party, by the will of Divine Providence, it was my fortune to have been a member.

I was born in Switzerland, in the Canton of Berne, December 18, 1810, and am now in my 77th year. My parents and my grand parents were Huguenots. My full name is Barbara Ann Shadecker (since Adams). My father's name was Samuel Shadecker.* He spoke the German and French tongues, and had been educated for a physician. He married Ann Kertz, also a native of Berne. To this couple were born five children, two girls and three boys. My brothers' names were John, Samuel and Christopher. My sister's name was Marianne. She was older than I.

LORD SELKIRK'S EMIGRATION SCHEME.

My father and mother were both Protestants in faith, and were devoted members of the Reformed Lutheran Church, in which belief they also raised their family. We always lived happily and contentedly in Berne until the year 1820, and supposed that the peaceful valleys of Switzerland were to be our home always. But this was not to be. In 1820, a person named Capt. Rudolph Mae, or Mai, came into that locality, and soon made himself known to the simple Swiss, by a flattering scheme which he proposed. Capt. Mae was a native of Berne, and had been some years in the military service of England, where he became acquainted with the Earl of Selkirk. Selkirk had been for some years engaged in a scheme of emigration, the object of which was to induce persons in Scotland and elsewhere, to remove to Rupert's Land in the center of North America, and form an agricultural colony there. This colony had been planted since

*Mrs. Adams spelled it thus. But in the records of the colony at Red River, the name is spelled *Scheidegger*, and *Scheidecker*.

1812, but the Scotch settlers from the **Highlands** and Orkneys whom he had induced to go there, were dissatisfied and many had left. He now conceived the idea of securing Swiss immigrants. Capt. Mae was entrusted with the work, and was well fitted for it, being a native of Berne himself, and speaking the language of its people. The Earl of Selkirk prepared and caused to be published in the French and German languages, a pamphlet giving a full, but over-colored description of the new country, its climate, soil and productions, and offered to all heads of families, or those who were unmarried and over twenty-one years of age, land free of cost, with seed, cattle and farming implements, all on a credit of three years. The route from Europe to the new colony, was to be *via* Hudson Bay, Nelson River, and Lake Winnipeg. The pamphlet alluded to, was freely distributed by Capt. Mae, and others of Lord Selkirk's agents, in the French-speaking cantons of Neuchatel, Vaud and Geneva, and in the German-speaking canton of Berne.

THE SWISS COLONISTS.

The false, but tempting accounts of the country, and the inducements held out to colonists, soon did their work, and shortly over 150 persons agreed to enroll in the party being made up. About three-fourths of these were French-speaking persons. All were Protestants, and generally intelligent and well-to do persons, some of them possessed of considerable means. Among them were several persons quite prominent in their communities, and who afterwards, in America, became citizens

—4

of repute and wealth. At the same time, it should be remembered, that but few of these adventurers were fitted for such a life as they were about to embark in. But a small number of them were agriculturists, and in general they were watchmakers, or skilled in some other branch of artizanship, totally unsuited to the wilderness into which they were going. My parents were among those captivated and seduced by this agent's glowing accounts and his promises, and after daily consulting together about the project, they concluded to go with the party which was soon to leave their native mountains for the distant and unknown spot in the new world, that seemed bright with promise for the poor Switzers. I was then but eleven years old, and little realized the importance of the fateful step which my parents were about being enticed into. At this very time (the summer of 1820) the Earl of Selkirk, the originator and promoter of this scheme, was already dead, but we did not know it for more than a year subsequently.

Considerable preparations were made by the colonists for the life in their new home. All of them invested what they could in goods and merchandise, to trade with in the new world. My father's intention was to establish himself as a weaver in Red River. A tan yard was another industry which some of the party made preparations for.*

---

*Abram Perret (or Perry), one of the earliest settlers of St. Paul, with his wife and four children, were among this party of Swiss immigrants.—J. F. W.

THE PARTY SETS OUT.

On May 3, 1821, the party of adventurers, not one of whom were ever to see their dear native mountains again, left Berne and other places near by, and assembled, to the number of 165 persons, at a small village on the Rhine near Basle. Why they did not assemble at Basle, which is a city of some commercial importance, seems a little strange. It was afterwards conjectured that the managers feared to take them to a large city, lest some unfavorable facts regarding the wild country to which they were being taken, should be communicated to them by persons who might have suspected that they were victims of deception, and would point out to them the fallacy of the promises and hopes which had engaged them in the enterprise. However this may have been, two large flat boats or barges were provided for their use at the point of embarkation above named, and in these they floated down the Rhine, delighted with its picturesque scenery, and the many historic spots and points along its banks. Still their hearts were burdened with the responsibilities of the important step they were about engaging in, and perhaps oppressed with grief at leaving their beautiful homes among the vine-clad hills and lovely valleys of dear Switzerland, one of the most beautiful countries of Europe. And the Switzers are a people who are proverbially attached to their homes. Yet, with their cheerful disposition and their strong religious faith, they bravely and hopefully looked forward to their future life in the new world as a realization of the dreams which all must have indulged in, of fortune and happiness greater than could ever come to them in the humble chalets of Helvetia.

THE OCEAN VOYAGE.

The voyage down the Rhine occupied ten days, when the colonists reached a small village, Dort, or Dordrecht, near Rotterdam, where the party embarked on the vessel *Lord Wellington*, and on May 30, 1821, cleared for Fort York, Hudson's Bay. After setting sail, their course lay east and north of Great Britain and just south of Greenland, to Hudson Strait. Soon after leaving Holland, the unpleasant discovery was made that the provisions issued to them were of quality greatly inferior to that stipulated before their departure. Complaint was duly made to the commander of the vessel about it—a stern, but kind hearted old seaman. The latter acknowledged that the complaint was just, but said that he was not responsible for it, which was doubtless true. The water was also bad, and issued in insufficient quantities. Arriving at Hudson Strait, latitude 62° north, the *Lord Wellington* overtook two English ships bound for Fort York, or York Factory, situated at the mouth of the Nelson river, laden with Indian goods and supplies for the garrisons at Forts York and Douglas, and for employes of the Hudson's Bay Company. The strait was filled with floes and bergs of ice, and the ships were thereby detained over three weeks. One day, in August, as the *Lord Wellington* lay moored alongside an ice field, a number of the passengers got out and danced on it. One of the supply ships was seriously damaged and nearly lost, by collision with an iceberg. Finally with much difficulty and no little peril, Hudson's Bay was entered, and after a long and tedious voyage of nearly four months, the wearied colonists were landed at Fort York, about Sept. 1st. Seven children had been born on the voyage out. As soon as "Mackinaw boats" could be procured, which took about a week, the party began the slow and toilsome ascent of the Nelson river.

FURTHER HARDSHIPS OF THE COLONISTS.

They had to propel their heavily laden boats, of which there was quite a fleet, by rowing, or poling, frequently against a very strong current, and, of course, proceeded slowly. Twenty days alone were occupied in the passage to Lake Winnipeg. Here they encountered further difficulties. The season was now quite advanced. The autumnal gales had set in, and their progress, skirting along the west shore of the lake, was slow and laborious. Head winds and high waves delayed them. They were frequently drenched with water, and chilled with cold. At night, hungry, fatigued, and benumbed with cold, we would land on some sheltered spot, prepare a camp, build fires, and make ourselves as comfortable as possible. In addition to our other troubles, our store of provisions ran short, and we were compelled to resort to fishing to keep from starving, but soon the supply of these was scanty. While we were traversing Lake Winnipeg, my brother Samuel, a boy, died suddenly. We stopped on an island and buried him hastily, not having anything to make a coffin of, even.

At the end of the third week, our party arrived, half

famished, at the mouth of Red River. Here more sad news awaited us. All the crops· of the colonists in the settlement, had been completely destroyed by grasshoppers, and the supply of breadstuffs which the colony had depended on for subsistence, thus destroyed. With heavy hearts, our party proceeded on up the Red River about thirty-five miles, to Fort Douglas, situated on the west bank of the river, below Fort Garry. This was then the principal trading post and headquarters of the Hudson's Bay Company. Governor Alexander McDowell, and other prominent officers of the company, were there at the time. They received us with kind and encouraging words, and what was of more importance to us just then, gave us a good supply of palatable food, and otherwise provided for our wants.

THE NEW COMERS HEAR BAD NEWS.

We here had an opportunity of conversing with some of the colonists and residents who had been here for some years, many, indeed, since 1818, when Selkirk's first colony had settled here. They did not give a very flattering account of life in the colony. They had all suffered great hardships. The climate was excessively severe, the winters long, and tho' the soil was rich, the shortness of the summers made it difficult to raise crops. Then there had been for several years past a cruel warfare between the two rival fur trading companies, the "Hudson Bay" and the "Northwest," and considerable blood-shed. This, however, they said, was now changed, by the consolidation of the two companies.

At this place, we heard another item of discouraging news, which, for some reason, had been concealed from us before. This was the death of Lord Selkirk, which had taken place, in fact, in April of the year preceding, in Europe. Still, as there was then only one mail per year to that distant point, brought by the annual expedition via Hudson Bay, with supplies for the posts, it may be that the officers of the company had not heard the news of Selkirk's death, until the arrival of their mails by the company's ships, which arrived simultaneously with us at Fort York. But it tended to further discourage the colonists, and to fill them with gloomy forebodings.

A SHARP COMPETITION FOR WIVES.

We had hardly landed at Fort Douglas, when a new sensation awaited us, which, in some of its features, was quite amusing, and a decided surprise to the colonists. It seems that there was quite a large class of men in the colony who went by the name of the "De Meurons." They had been recruited in Canada by Lord Selkirk, several years before, to act as soldiers in the hostilities mentioned a moment ago, and were (if I remember correctly) called *De Meurons* because their commander had borne that name. After the hostilities were over, and the men discharged, Lord Selkirk induced many of them to settle on lands which he donated to them, around Fort Douglas. They all became well-to-do farmers, but were without wives, a very necessary help-meet to farmers, and were all anxious to obtain them, but that was out of the question in the colony. When they heard that a colony of Swiss settlers were coming, with a number of females, they resolved to repair to the Fort on its arrival and endeavor to secure partners. We had not been at this place more than 24 hours, before the De Meurons, notified of our arrival, began to flock in, each eager to get a wife. And some were very eager. They went at it without any hesitation or backwardness. On finding a maiden that suited their fancy, they would open negotiations at once, either with her or her parents, and would not take any refusal. I saw an amusing incident during this matrimonial fair. An eager De Meuron seized a woman by the hand, saying, "I want to marry you," but was much disappointed when she told him, "I have a husband." The result of this aggressive onset was, that not a few of the De Meurons did get wives among the families of the settlers, and generally both parties were suited. My sister was one who thus consented to share the lot of a Red River farmer. The weddings were celebrated with as much gaiety as was possible, considering the circumstances of both the colonists and the settlers.

The elders of our company (for we children did not understand much of these troubles), soon began to realize into what a predicament they had come, and there were heavy hearts and sad countenances. Governor McDowell plainly told the newly arrived emigrants that there were not provisions enough in the Colony to carry them all through the winter, and the problem seemed for a time to be a very serious one. After some consultation, it was deemed best to divide the party. He directed that about seventy-five of the youngest and strongest should proceed about sixty miles farther up the river, to a place called Pembina, on the United States side of the boundary line (though then supposed to be north of that line), where it was believed that game, such as buffalo, elk, deer, fish, etc.. were more abundant, and where a good supply of "pemmican" could be obtained from the Indians and half-breeds in that locality.

THE COLONISTS PASS A HARD WINTER.

This was consequently carried into effect. My father's family was one of those selected to go to Pembina, and we proceeded thither, arriving just at the beginning of winter. Here father secured a habitation, such as it was, but it at least gave us a shelter. But we were ab-solutely destitute of food, and winter was just commenc-ing with all the severity known in that climate. For-tunately, my father had money, and he at once hired two Indians to hunt buffaloes. We soon had an abundance of meat, and lived on that kind of food as long as we remained there. Sometimes his Indians had to bring it a long distance, but fortunately our supply did not fail us, most of the time, although at one period, when there had been very deep snows, we were three days without food. Another privation was, that we had no salt, and were compelled to eat our buffalo meat without it.

There was a post of the Hudson's Bay Company near there, and when our food gave out, my father applied there to purchase some. The agent was absent, and his wife absolutely refused to sell him any. But during the argument, she espied a handsome gold watch which my mother carried, and demanded that in return for the food needed. Although its intrinsic value was considerable, it was prized more on account of its associations, and my parents were reluctant to give it up. But they at length yielded to necessity, and gave the watch for the food, it being many fold greater in value than what we received for it.

After some time of enduring these hardships, my father heard of a place down the river some ways, where we would doubtless fare better, and had us taken there in dog sleds. We were two days in going there, and had to camp out at night, in the snow, with nothing to eat but buffalo broth. The place to which we went, was a trading post. There was a house there, where the owner rented us one room, in which we lived the balance of the winter. We had nothing to sleep on but buffalo robes, but we had abundance of food, and thus got along very well. The cold now began to be intense. It was said to be the severest winter known for years. At night the trees would crack, with the fierce cold, like the reports of guns. But we passed the rest of the winter without any serious discomfort.

THE SEASON OF 1822.

In the spring of the next year (1822), the two sections of the colony were again united, and land having been apportioned to them, under the original agreement made by Selkirk's agents, they all commenced to make settlements, near Fort Garry, and erect houses. The location chosen by my father was about three miles above Fort Garry, on the Red River, where he had a log house built for him. He was engaged in partnership in his farm enterprise with a Mr. Fletcher, an Englishman. I may here remark that not one of us could, at that time, speak a word of English, and we experienced considerable difficulty on that account. The agriculture carried on by the Swiss settlers that season was of a very limited and·rude sort. Not one of them had any plow cattle, and what little they raised was done by˙ digging the ground merely. But we lived more comfortably than before, and now had hopes that our rash move in coming to that region would not prove so disastrous to our fortunes and happiness as we had, at first arrival, supposed.   We all entered somewhat into the life of the settlement. I soon learned to paddle a canoe, to fish, and to swim. On June 10, 1822, my sister, Marianna, was married (as I before mentioned) to a Mr. Mathias Schmidt, by the Rev. John West, an English Episcopal clergyman, well known in the settlement.

THE DISCONTENT OF THE SWISS SETTLERS.

The poor Swiss colonists, who had been beguiled into making their homes in that region, were not long in getting their eyes opened to the fact that their credulity had made them the dupes of the agents of Lord Selkirk. Though some of them were poor in their former hcmes, they had at least comfortable dwellings, and occupations which would give them bread. Here they had nothing to look forward to but destitution, trouble and toil.   My father kept up a brave heart through it all, although his scanty means were being gradually consumed. His strong religious faith was one thing which sustained him. Every night he would gather his family together, and after reading the Sacred Scriptures, pray with great fervor to our heavenly Father for help and guidance. He never lost faith in a kind and over-ruling Providence, in the darkest hours we experienced, while living in the Red River settlements.

The winter passed by the Swiss colonists at Pembina, had been one of great hardship. It was a winter of unusual severity, and the snow much deeper than had been known for years. This latter fact sometimes almost cut off their supplies of meat. They were compelled to fish through holes iu the ice, and even Indian dogs were bought and eaten! Several settlers were maimed for life by the freezing of their hands and feet.

Several families, disheartened at their privations, and finding that the supplies of cattle, etc., promised them, were not forthcoming, resolved to leave the Red River region at all hazards. Five families got away in the fall of 1821, and reached Fort Snelling in safety, where they were permitted to settle on the military reservation. A general discontent prevailed among all the Swiss. There were only a very few who, by some fortunate chance, had got a good location, and felt encouraged enough to remain and "stick it out." Even most of these left after a few years, and went to Minnesota. Among them was Abram Perret and family, Joseph Rondo, Benj. and Pierre Gervais, Louis Massie, and others, who left after the great flood of 1826, and subsequently settled at St. Paul. My father's means, which he had brought with him, were gradually becoming exhausted, and destitution would soon have stared us in the face. The summer of 1822 was another year of crop failure, owing to the grasshopper scourge, and it seemed that the cup of our afflictions was full. My father, during this winter, resolved to leave at all hazards, for Fort Snelling the next spring, and others had also made the same resolve.

THEY RESOLVE TO ABANDON RED RIVER.

Consequently, in the spring of 1823, as soon as the grass was grown sufficiently, father and his family, with twelve other Swiss families, started for Fort Snelling. There were twelve men and a boy in the party, who were generally well armed; all the rest were women and children, one or two of the latter being infants in arms. We had hired several "Red River Carts," drawn by oxen, which carried our provisions etc., and of course every body had to walk, except, perhaps, some of the younger children, who rode occasionally, and one or two men, who had horses. Two or three of the women carried babes in their arms, walking thus twenty miles per day. We followed the trail on the west side of the Red River, over the prairie. Two mounted guides accompanied us (the drivers of the carts), who could speak the Sioux language, in case we met any Indians, and act as hunters, to supply us with food. They killed several buffalo on the way. Our habit was to camp out at night, and we always had a guard carefully patrol our camp during these bivouacs. Very often the women would thus stand guard, in order to allow the men to rest. Several times we met parties of Indians, whose good will we had to conciliate by giving them presents of food, ammunition, or trinkets, a small supply of which we had brought for that purpose. They did not seem to desire to injure us in any way, but when we reached Fort Snelling, a few weeks subsequently, we learned that, on the very road we had traversed, they had just killed part of

a family who, like ourselves, had been on their way from
Pembina to Fort Snelling.

THE TULLY FAMILY.

This was a family named Tully.　Mr. Tully was a
Scotchman, and a blacksmith by occupation, who, like many
others, had been living at the Red River settlement, and
had got starved out.　He had started a few weeks before
our party, to go to Fort Snelling, and very unwisely went
alone.　He was met near what is now Grand Forks, by
some Sioux, who demanded of him to give up his provisions.　Of course, to do this. would be to leave his family
to perish, so he refused.　The Indians then killed him, and
his wife, and also a little baby.　John and Andrew Tully,
two boys, attempted to escape, but were pursued and
caught, when one of the Indians partially scalped John,
but the rest interfered and they took both prisoners.　Col.
Snelling, hearing of it, sent persons to rescue them, and
the boys were taken to Fort Snelling, where they were
when we arrived.　They were cared for by Col. Snelling
in his family.　John Tully soon after died, but the other,
(Andrew) grew up as an inmate of Col. Snelling's family,
and is now living in an eastern city.

TROUBLE FROM THE INDIANS.

We had several bad frights from Indians, however.　One
evening we were camped on the Bois de Sioux River,
shortly below its exit from Lake Traverse, when I
stepped down to the edge with a pail to get some water.
I heard noise on the opposite bank, and limbs crackle; a
dog also barked.　I was certain it was Indians, and slip-

ping back quietly to the camp, I told the men what I had heard. They carefully scouted in the direction named, but saw nothing. But they suspected some ambuscade, and resolved on a plan to baffle the red skins. They built a large fire, and stuffing some men's clothes with grass, to resemble human forms, laid them by the fire, so that if the savages really were lying in wait to attack us, they would fire into these supposed bodies, and thus get baffled. They did not, however, attack us, and it is probable were only endeavoring to steal some of our horses.

Near Fort Traverse, a trading post on the Lake of that name, some Indians overtook us on a prairie. They were on horseback. We had just crossed the river by fording. They were angry with us for killing buffalo. The Indians rode along with us a little distance, and just then some one noticed that one of them had disappeared. We feared some treachery, and kept a close lookout. We saw that we were approaching an Indian village, still some distance off. Apparently some signal had been given, for a number of mounted Indians came riding towards us, firing guns, not at us, but in the air. They got to us, and at once mounted the carts, and threw everything out. A young Indian caught hold of me, and being alarmed, I started and ran. He pursued me some distance, I do not know why, when a chief, as I presumed him to be, rode up, and probably ordered him to desist, as he stopped. This same chief harangued the warriors, and doubtless commanded them to desist, as they ceased any further demonstrations against us. The same Indians followed us to Fort Traverse. We were compelled to give them a considerable ransom. Father gave them one horse. They did not molest us any farther, and even sent two Indians with us for some distance, to notify other bands we might meet, not to harm us. While we were with them they showed us an old battle field where some of their tribe had been killed. One of our carts ran over a bare place on this spot, which seemed to enrage them. It had some significance which we could not understand. We camped near this spot, and the Indians howled all night.

THEY DESCEND THE ST. PETER'S RIVER.

It now began to be late in the fall. The families who were with us, the Moniers, the Chetlains, Schirmers, Langets, and others, being anxious to reach Fort Snelling before navigation should close, so that they could go on down the river, hurried on ahead, leaving father and his family to finish the rest of the voyage alone. Our destination was Fort Snelling. We at once made for a trading house on the Minnesota River, where father and my oldest brother built, after some delay and hard labor, for they could not get the proper tools, a big dug-out, of a cottonwood log. Into this we embarked all that we had left, provisions, clothing, etc. The carts, and their drivers, who had brought us so far, now left us, and returned to the Red River settlement, and we pushed off, in our rude pirogue, down the Minnesota River, then called "the St. Peter's." The river was quite low, and we experienced considerable trouble in getting over, or around, sand bars, or shoals. Such was the slowness of our progress that it was quite late in the season when we reached Fort Snelling.   In fact, ice was already floating in the river before we concluded our trip.

The other party of refugees, had, after a brief stay at Fort Snelling, been provided by Col. Snelling with provisions and boats, in which they started off as soon as possible, down the Mississippi.   (Steamboats had reached Fort Snelling for the first time that year, but their trips were few and far between.)   The colonists mostly went to St. Louis and made their homes there, though some went as far as Vevay, Ind.   In a couple of years, most of those at St. Louis went to the newly opened lead regions at and near Galena, and became prosperous citizens.   My father and mother joined the party at that place subsequently.   Descendants of this party are scattered all over the west, many of them having attained distinction.   General A. L. Chetlain, of Galena. who was associated with Gen. Grant in the war, was the son of Louis Chetlain. one of this party of refugees.

THE ARRIVAL AT FORT SNELLING.

We landed at the Fort with a feeling of joy and gratitude.   Our journey through the great wilderness which stretched between Fort Garry and Fort Snelling, was one of fatigue, danger and privation; it had consumed nearly five months.   We now felt that we had gotten into a land where we could live with comfort, and in the hope of a happy future, a condition we could not look forward to in the Selkirk settlement.   The trials, hardships and anxieties through which we had passed the past two or three years had told visibly on my dear parents.

—5

Both of them had aged rapidly, and it had sowed in the
constitutions of both the seeds of premature decay, which
shortened their lives.

FORT SNELLING IN 1823.

Col. Snelling, to whom my father applied for permis-
sion to remain on the Military Reservation, very kindly
acceded to our request, and expressed much sympathy
for us, ordering that provisions should be issued to us,
although there was a scarcity in the garrison at that
time, for some cause, (a miscalculation on the part of
the commander as to what amount was necessary, I believe,) and the troops were actually on half rations. A
part of the old barracks at " Coldwater," as it was
called, was assigned for our occupancy, and we installed
ourselves there. and made ourselves as comfortable as
possible, under the circumstances. Father got some em-
ployment on the reservation, and Mrs. Snelling, a kind
and benevolent lady, gave me a home in her family,
where I aided her in the care of her little children, a
task for which I was well fitted, as I was now 13 years
of age, and very strong and active. Thus, again, fortune smiled on us, and we began to take fresh hope,
after all our trials and losses. I had a comfortable and
pleasant home in Mrs. Snelling's family. Both she and
the Colonel treated me with the greatest kindness, and
the children soon became greatly attached to me, so
that my position in the Snelling family was a really en-·'
viable one. I think of those days as among the happiest
of my life, and feel thankful for my good fortune.

Fort Snelling was not, at that time, completely finished, but was occupied. Col. Snelling had sowed some wheat that season, and had it ground at a mill which the government had built at the falls, but the wheat had become mouldy, or sprouted, and made wretched, black, bitter tasting bread. This was issued to the troops, who got mad because they could not eat it, and brought it to the parade ground and threw it down there. Col. Snelling came out and remonstrated with them. There was much inconvenience that winter (1823–24) about the scarcity of provisions. Some of the soldiers had the scurvy, and I believe some died. Whiskey rations were issued to the troops regularly, however, and sometimes it seemed that about all they had was whiskey. These troops were a part of the Fifth Infantry. Adjt. Green's little boy died at the fort while I was there, and was buried in the cemetery attached to the fort. Several soldiers were also buried there, during the period I lived in the fort, and a regular military funeral was given each of them, the band playing a dirge, and their company firing volleys over their graves.

THE SNELLING FAMILY.

The names of the Snelling children living then were Henry, James, Josiah and Marian. They had lost some others prior to the time I had lived with them, but the above grew up to adult age. James became a captain in the U. S. Army and died in 1855; Josiah is, or was some time ago, a physician in Illinois; Marian married a Mr. Hazard and lives in Newport, Ky.; Henry Hunt Snelling was quite an able writer and poet.

Mrs. Snelling was a very fond and indulgent mother, and spared no pains or sacrifices to make her children happy. As there were no schools at the Fort, she taught them herself, as well as she could. I taught them the prayers which my parents had taught to me. Col. Snelling also had a son, by a first wife, who lived with us a part of the time. He was then (1823) about twenty years old. His name was William Joseph, or Wm. Josiah Snelling; they called him "Jo" usually. Mrs. Snelling did not seem to have any great fondness or respect for him, and perhaps with good reasons; but the Colonel was greatly attached to him, and would do anything for him. Jo. led rather an ungoverned life for some years. He had been at one time appointed a Cadet at West Point, and a son of Maj. Hamilton, of Fort Snelling, was there at the same time. These lads committed some breach of discipline while at the military academy, and were sent home. Mrs. Hamilton was much distressed at this, and wept profusely. Jo. Snelling married, while quite young, a French girl from Prairie du Chien, very handsome, but uneducated. They lived in a sort of hovel for awhile, and, owing to cold and privation during the ensuing winter, the poor girl took sick and died. After this, he returned to Fort Snelling, and thence went to lake Traverse, where he was engaged in the Indian trade. He subsequently went to Boston, married again there, and died a few years later. Jo. somewhat resembled the Colonel in person, but his hair was darker. The Colonel's hair was quite red. He was also slightly bald. From this peculiarity the soldiers nick-named him, among themselves, the "prairie-hen." Once Jo. told his father of this. The Colonel laughed at it as a good joke.

GARRISON LIFE DESCRIBED.

Intemperance, among both officers and men, at that time, was an almost universal thing, and produced deplorable effects. I regret to say that the commandant was no exception to this rule. Usually kind and pleasant, when one of his convivial spells occurred, he would act furious, sometimes getting up in the night and making a scene. He was severe in his treatment of the men who committed a like indiscretion. He would take them to his room, and compel them to strip, when he would flog them unmercifully. I have heard them beg him to spare them, "for God's sake." Col. S. was quite improvident in his habits, and usually in debt. One time, old Mr. Spalding, who had been employed in the Commissary service for some years, and had saved several hundred dollars, mostly in silver, brought it to Col. Snelling, and asked him to take care of it for him. Col. S. said he would. After Col. Snelling's death, Mr. Spalding used to declare that it had never been returned to him.

SOCIETY AT THE FORT.

During my sojourn at Fort Snelling, of six years, I had opportunity to become acquainted with nearly all the officers of the Fifth Infantry stationed there during that period (1823-29). Among those whose names I can now remember, were Col. Josiah Snelling, Surgeon J. P. C. McMahon, Maj. Joseph C. Plympton, Maj. Thomas Hamilton, Maj. Nathan Clark, Captains Watkins, Wm. E. Cruger, St. Clair Denny, De Lafayette Wilcox, and Lieutenants Robert A. McCabe, David Hunker, J. B. F. Russell, Joseph M. Bayley, Melancthon Smith, Wm. E.

Cruger, Platt R. Green, Louis T Jamison, etc. I believe that not a single one of the above are living now. Many of these officers were men of the highest ability, most of them having been graduates of West Point. Several of them, unfortunately, contracted social habits in the army which ultimately clouded the honor which they would otherwise have won from their meritorious military careers, and more than one of them closed his days even in disgrace and poverty. Army life was not favorable to saving money; no officer that I ever knew made any money while in the army. There was less blame to be attached to their error in the way of conviviality, than there would have been to men in other occupations. Garrison life at Ft. Snelling and other frontier posts, those days, was a very monotonous round of existence. The routine duties of the day consumed but very little time, ordinarily, and the rest of the time must have hung very heavy on their hands. In summer they could amuse themselves with hunting, as game was always abundant. But during the long and rigorous winters it was a great problem, "how to kill time." Card playing and drinking thus came into an unfortunate prominence. This some times resulted in disputes and quarrels, which, in several cases, led to duels between officers. Two or three of these meetings occurred while I was there. I do not now remember the names of those who took part in them, but I can recall that they made considerable talk and excitement at the time.

Nearly every officer I have named was married, and in almost every case to ladies of the best families, and who were endowed with beauty and many accomplishments.

Thus the society at the Fort at that period was of the most select and aristocratic. Many of these ladies would have shone in any circle. Their households in the garrison were attractive places, and showed evidences of wealth and good taste. I remember that Mrs. Maj. Plympton brought the first piano to Fort Snelling, which was brought to Minnesota. I knew Mrs. Maj. Clarke well. She was the mother of Mrs. Van Cleve, and was an amiable and lovely woman. I remember the latter (Charlotte Clarke) when she was "a little tot," three or four years old, playing near the door of her father's quarters. She used to play with the Snelling children, who were in my care. When Gen. Scott visited the Fort in 1826 there was a great striving to do him honor. The resources of the larder were limited, at Fort Snelling, those days, but everything possible was done that ingenuity suggested. He was a guest of Col. Snelling, and the spread was a creditable one. All the officers and their wives were present at his reception in full dress. Many of the ladies wore blazing diamonds. But the dressmaker was an institution not at hand in those days. Opportunities for frequent renewals of wardrobe were scanty. The arrivals of steamboats, which brought supplies from the states, were few and far between, even in the summer time. Of course there were weeks in the winter time when there was not even a mail. The latter were brought by "dog-train" from Prairie du Chien, or in some such way, at rare intervals.

My parents had lived at Fort Snelling some two years when they concluded to remove to the Galena lead mines, where most of the other Swiss colonists had settled, and were doing well. Father soon after died there, and mother returned to the Fort to live with me. My brothers grew up, and lived in Wisconsin. John, the eldest, died at Fort Howard, Green Bay, where he was a trader. Chris., the younger, died in the army during the rebellion.

VARIOUS INCIDENTS OF FORT LIFE.

The Indians used to bring buffalo meat to the Fort, and sell it to the soldiers, and others, who relished it greatly, as the meat issued to them for rations, was always salt. Once an ox got drowned in the river near the Fort, and the Indians got its body, and cutting it up, sold it to the soldiers as buffalo meat. When the soldiers found out how ' they had been hoaxed, they were furiously mad.

A Mr. Camp was once stopping at Col. Snelling's house, was taken sick and died there. He had either been an officer, or perhaps connected with the sutler's store. He was buried in the cemetery near the Fort, and the band played at his funeral.

Two men of Capt. McCabe's company once quarreled, and one stabbed the other with a butcher's knife, so that he died. The murdered man was an' Englishman. I understood that no punishment was ever meted to the one who killed him—why, I never learned.

A man named Angell came to the Fort from Red River while I was there and had in his possession a considerable quantity of gold, which he buried, for safety. He was, not long after, taken sick, and died. He tried to tell those who were with him, where it was, but could not. So his gold slept in the ground for over fifty years, and was discovered not long ago by some laborers digging for foundations of the new buildings for the post. Burying money was common those days, as there were no banks, or even safes to keep it in securely.

Once a soldier and his wife, both young people, were found to be making and circulating bogus money. He was drummed out of the service and both sent adrift from the fort in a canoe. I have often wondered at the fate of those persons. There was not a human habitation between Fort Snelling and Prairie du Chien, and I have thought they may have perished from hunger and exposure.

At various times members of the families of officers at the fort died there and were buried in the military cemetery. Adjt. Green lost a child thus, and also Lt. Melancthon Smith. Mrs. Snelling buried at least one there, and the cemetery there in time contained quite a group of graves. Headstones were erected to most of them, but after the families would move away to other parts, the graves were generally neglected.

I remember also seeing Count Beltrami, the Italian, who came to Fort Snelling in 1823. He had been up to Red River, and on his return stopped at the fort some time. He could not speak English, but could speak French. He was at Mrs. Snelling's a great deal, and Mrs. Snelling could converse with him in French: she had been studying it under the tuition of an old soldier belonging to the garrison.

Major Taliaferro, the Indian agent, was another of the characters well known at the fort. Hardly a day passed without delegates of Indians of some tribe or other visiting him and having a grand palaver with him. Thus parties of them were encamped almost constantly near the fort. Sometimes these were of hostile tribes, and fights very frequently took place between them.

A PERILOUS JOURNEY IN EARLY DAYS.

In the summer of 1825, Col. and Mrs. Snelling with their children, and the Tully boys made a trip to Detroit to pay a visit to her relatives, the Hunts and McIntoshes, at that place.* I accompanied them on that journey, and it had some features which are worth relating. Our mode of conveyance to Prairie du Chien, was in Mackinaw boats, with soldiers for crew. We had to camp every night, which was not very pleasant at all times, as it rained frequently, and the mosquitos were excessively troublesome. Adjt. Green accompanied us. One day he lost his military hat, in the river, and could not recover it. I loaned him a sun bonnet which I had, and rather than go bare-headed to Prairie du Chien, the nearest place where he could buy another hat, he wore it during the whole river trip. But there was no one to make fun of him, for we saw not a soul, white men or women, that is, on the whole route. In gratitude for this favor, when we reached Mackinaw, he purchased me a handsome bonnet.

When we reached Prairie du Chien, we put up at Fort Crawford, and tarried there a day or two, to rest.

*Mrs. Ellet in her memoir of Mrs. Snelling, in "Pioneer Women of the West." p. 330, gives a somewhat fanciful account of this trip. Mrs. Adams' account is far more minute, and undoubtedly more correct.   W.

The Snellings were guests of Col. and Mrs. Zachary
Taylor, who were stationed there then. It was a daugh-
ter of this couple which Jefferson Davis married, while
a lieutenant in the army. I fell sick here, and wanted
to return home, i. e., to the Fort. There was really
nothing the matter with me but home-sickness. I had
never been separated from my parents before. Mrs.
Snelling was alarmed, as she did not know what to do
unless I accompanied her on the journey, to care for
the children. She talked about it with Mrs. Taylor.
That lady came to see me. She was a fat, motherly
looking woman. She told Mrs. Snelling the best way
was to divert me and I would soon forget my ailment.
This was done, and the cure succeeded.

We soon resumed our voyage, this time up the Wisconsin river, still in our Mackinaw boats. But it was
more tedious now, as it was up stream. The soldiers
rowed and poled, and had very fatiguing work to get
us along, and it was very slow, at times. Mrs. Snelling stood the fatigues of the trip well. We had the
best cooks along, who prepared our meals in good style.
We passed over the portage between the Wisconsin and
Fox rivers, and then down the latter, to Green Bay,
where we embarked on a schooner for Detroit, which
we reached safely.

We spent several weeks with the Hunts, at Detroit,
and late in the fall started on our homeward trip, and
retraced the same route we came. From Prairie du
Chien, we ascended the river in keel boats. The one
in which the Col, and his family were, had a very com
fortable cabin. There was a crew of eight or ten men

We took in at Prairie du Chien the Colonel's son, Jo, and also an Indian trader, going to the Sioux river. He was attacked with the ague. Mrs. Snelling nursed and doctored him as well as she was able, but there was really nothing on board that could be given him—not even whiskey.

Our progress up stream was very slow, although the crew toiled hard. The weather began to get cold and stormy, and it seemed that winter was approaching fast. Our supply of provisions began to look ominously small; we actually were reduced to corn. Above Lake Pepin the ice stopped us once, and during a gale of wind, the boat was driven fast among some trees. The Col. said, "it looks as if we would have to stay here for good." The men pulled hard. Even Mrs. Snelling and I helped at the ropes. Night came on cold and tempestuous. Finally, the men went ashore and built a fire, and prepared to pass the night as best they could. The women and children remained in the cabin. At night the boat sprung a leak, having been injured by the ice, and the water poured in, frightening us badly, as we expected the boat was about to sink. The wind was still roaring and the waves beating against us noisily. It was at this place, or very near here where it had been reported that the Indians, a few days before had killed two white men, and chopped them to pieces. Col. Snelling uncautiously mentioned this, and that again increased our terror.

Early next morning the Colonel dispatched his son Jo, and a soldier named Butterfield afoot to the Fort for help. They both knew the country well, and were used to bushwhacking. Some parched corn was all the provisions our cook could supply them with, so reduced our stores had become. Each had an ax and a blanket, nothing more.

The Col. now rallied the men and bailed the boat out, when we got it loosened from the trees, and crossed the river, where we were in a sheltered place. Here the boat sank. Fortunately, the water was shallow, and we got out all the contents and carried them ashore. The men now made a rude hut or tent of poles, etc., and we (the women and children) made the most of this uncomfortable bivouac. Among the stores that was left was a barrel of cider. The Col. had hoped to take this home to the fort, where it would have been a welcome treat to his fellow officers, but unperceived by him, some of the men slyly tapped it, and were commencing to show signs of intoxication, when he detected the joke, and to avoid any further trouble, stove in the barrel with an ax. Amid all our trials, the Col. was merry and light-hearted and was continually cracking jokes at our expense.

Jo. Snelling and Butterfield, as it subsequently turned out, were unable to pursue their journey far. They came to a river (the St. Croix?) which they could not cross, although they made some attempt to construct a raft. Not long after they had left us, the Colonel started two more men for the Fort, on the other side of the river, so as to double our chances of securing help speedily. These scouts arrived at the Fort safely, and two mackinaw boats were at once started off to our relief, with provisions, etc. Unfortunately, the ice had gorged at a narrow place in the river, (perhaps above Hastings,) and the boats were thus blockaded there. One or two of this crew then started off to meet us, carrying sacks of bread and meat.

All this had taken some time, and we were still in our wretched tent, hungry and shivering. It seemed the best way to go on and meet the expected relief, so as to hasten the time when we would receive it. Our men carried the tent and what other necessaries we had to have, and we started off on our painful and slow journey up the river. When night came we had not made much advance, and again camped by the river, where a huge fire helped to warm and cheer us. That night was as near an experience of being homeless and foodless as any of us ever wanted to realize. The long night wore away, and when the dull, cold morning dawned, we ate what scanty food we had, and again started on our weary tramp. All that sustained us in this painful march was the thought that it was a matter of life or death for us; that if we did not soon meet the expected relief we would perish of cold and hunger.

Hour after hour passed by, and it must have been after noon when we were electrified by a cry of "they're coming, they're coming." The help had come, and we were saved. The bags of meat and bread were quickly attacked, and we soon satisfied our hunger. Mrs. Snelling and I cried for joy. Johnny ·Tully said, "what fools you are to cry now. Why didn't you cry when we were in danger of starving?"

Encouraged and strengthened, we soon reached where boats were awaiting us, and started in them, with hearts sensibly lighter, up the stream. It was still many miles to the Fort, and night came on us sooner than we expected. We were again compelled to camp out as best we could, but this was not esteemed such a hardship, as we knew we were so near home. That night there was a violent storm of snow and wind, and our tent was once blown down. The next morning the snow was quite deep. Just then two sleighs met us, which had been sent from the fort to hasten our arrival. The Colonel and his family and I mounted in these, and we started off. There were no roads, however, and our progress was very slow. We upset four times, and did not arrive at the Fort until after dark. Mr. and Mrs. Clarke had a good, warm supper ready for us when we arrived. The garrison fired a cannon salute when the Colonel drove in the gate, and there was great rejoicing at our safety.

His first act was to inquire about Jo. and Butterfield, who had not arrived. The Col. was very uneasy, and dispatched scouts in search of them, with directions to fire shots every few minutes. They were found in due time, almost famished, and brought in safely.

The Col. was much impressed by our escape from the dangers encountered, and said he recognized the hand of Providence in it. He became quite religious, and had prayers in his family for some time, but little by little the conviviality and worldliness of garrison life effaced these impressions, and we saw no more of them.

INDIAN HOSTILITIES AND ITS RESULT.

The year 1827 witnessed some exciting events. I mentioned before, that parties of the Ojibwas and Dakotas, two intensely hostile tribes, used to encamp at the same time near the Fort, and that collisions occurred between them from that cause. In May, that year, a disturbance of this kind happened, that was of more than usual importance and note. A considerable party of Ojibwas, and several Dakotas, were encamped near the Fort, and the Dakotas treacherously sent proposals of peace and friendship to the Ojibwas. The latter accepted them, and several of the Dakotas, armed, visited the wigwam of their chief, and were there hospitably entertained and feasted. They withdrew after a time, but on getting outside the lodge, turned and fired a volley into it and wounded eight of the Ojibwa inmates, of whom a part died of their wounds. Col. Snelling and Maj. Taliaferro, the Indian agent, had before strongly charged on these savages that no hostilities would be permitted within the area around the Fort, that it would be an insult to the United States flag. When this last cowardly act occurred, he at once notified them that they must make ample reparation. Several were put under arrest, and held as hostages until the real murderers, who had fled, should be delivered up. Runners were at once sent out to the villages, and in a day or two, four of the Dakota culprits were in the guard house awaiting their fate, and were identified as the guilty persons. Col. Snelling, after consulting with the other officers, as to what way he could make an example of them, agreed to leave it to the Ojibwas. The latter proposed that the Sioux murderers be made to ''run the gauntlet;'' that is the Ojibwas should be stationed on the prairie, with loaded guns, and the Dakotas placed a few yards off, and told to run. If they could escape unharmed, well and well, but the Ojibwas would do their best to kill them. This was all carried out, as planned. The place chosen was just outside the Fort, on the level prairie, but the Colonel would not permit any of the garrison to go out and witness it. He said it was an Indian trouble entirely—the whites had nothing to do with it. Mrs. Snelling and I got up on the roof of their house, and thus had a clear view of it all. It was a lovely warm bright May morning. I remember the whole scene as if it had been yesterday.

The Ojibwas tied the arms of the three Dakota murderers, and led them out 30 yards. When the signal was given, the Dakotas bounded off like deer. The guns cracked, and soon all three of the culprits leaped into the air and fell, either dead, or dying. One of these was a great coward, and showed signs of the most mortal terror. The other two had been brave and defiant, and sang a war song when the Ojibwas were tying them. They also upbraided the cowardly one.

When the victims fell, the Ojibwas gave their scalp cry, rushed up to the two brave dead ones, scalped them, and dipping their fingers in the gushing blood from their wounds, licked and sucked them. Some caught the blood in the hollow of their hand and drank it. This made their faces look bloody and horrible, and they looked wild and savage like demons. The body of the cowardly one was not noticed, nor did they drink his blood. Colonel Snelling then went out and told the Ojibwas they must not leave the bodies lying there, and they must drag them away. They took the corpses by the heels and dragging them to the steep bank of the river above the fort, threw them over into the water. It chanced that there was a large tree on the bank, blown over into the water. They took the Indian that had not been scalped and tied his hair to one of the limbs of this tree, in

—6

the water. For several days it rocked up and down by the motion of the waves, exposing the ghastly face of the dead to sight every moment or two. I saw it several times as I was going along the bank to visit my sister, and it horrified me. I spoke to Mrs. Snelling about it, and she got the Colonel to have some one dislodge the body and let it float off.*

THE MILITARY EXPEDITION TO PRAIRIE DU CHIEN.

In July, 1827, some murders committed by drunken Winnebagoes on settlers near Prairie du Chien, created a great panic in that region, and the whites rushed into old Fort Crawford, to take refuge and protect themselves. I should have observed, before, that in the fall of the previous year, Fort Crawford had been measurably abandoned, and the two or three companies of the Fifth U. S. Infantry which it contained, had been sent to Fort Snelling, making that garrison very full. There was, really, no danger that the Winnebagoes would attack the people entrenched in Fort Crawford, because their spree was already over, and everything had got quieted down, but all the whites were so panic-stricken and alarmed, that an express was sent to Col. Snelling, imploring him to send down relief at once. Of course, Col. Snelling could not refuse this appeal. He at once hurried off with four companies, in keel-boats, and several days afterward, several more companies followed,

---

*A very interesting account of this incident, undoubtedly written by Wm. J. Snelling, will be found in the collections of this society, vol. 1, p. 439. Another account, written by Mrs. C. O. Van Cleve, is given in vol. 3, p. 76. The account given by Mrs. Adams is very similar to the two foregoing. Beyond doubt, Mrs. Van Cleve and Mrs. Adams, are the only two persons now living, who witnessed the interesting event.   W.

under one of the other regimental officers, leaving Fort Snelling almost deserted.

Mrs. Snelling and the children went with the Colonel, and I accompanied them. The upshot of the whole expedition was, that not a hostile Indian was seen on the whole trip, and not a shot was fired. The troops simply "marched down the hill," and then "marched back again." Two of the Winnebagoes, called Red Bird and Wee-Kau, were apprehended and imprisoned on charge of murder, and if I remember aright, were sentenced to be hung, but it was, I think, never done, for fear of arousing an outbreak of the tribe. [Mrs. Adams was misinformed. The Indians were executed.]

The expedition to Prairie du Chien had quite an important turn for myself, because, while there, I was united in marriage to Joseph Adams, who was an officer in the Ordnance department at Fort Snelling, and accompanied the troops on their expedition. Mr. Adams was a native of Derbyshire, Eng., and was a true model of a manly soldier in every respect. I had known him at Fort Snelling, and highly respected him for his fine qualities. Our married life was an extremely happy one. We returned to Fort Snelling in a few days after our marriage, and lived there over two years.

THE FIFTH REGIMENT GOES TO ST. LOUIS.

In the fall of this year (1827) the Fifth Regiment was ordered to Jefferson Barracks, at Saint Louis. Colonel Snelling proceeded to Washington in August, to attend to some business there, and while in that city, was seized with inflammation of the brain, and died suddenly, on

Aug. 28. His death was a terrible blow to Mrs. Snelling, and a source of grief to all of us who knew him. I had been an inmate of his family for four years, and his kindness to me had made me greatly attached to him. I parted with his sorrowing family, soon after, feeling that I had lost my best friends.

SAULT STE MARIE, AND NOTABLES THERE.

My husband and I went to Jefferson Barracks with the Fifth Regiment in 1827, and not long after reaching there my mother died. From this post, we were transferred to Detroit, and then to Fort Brady, at Sault Ste Marie, where we remained some time. At this place there were a few quite notable characters, that interested me very much. Henry R. Schoolcraft was Indian agent there at that time. I became well acquainted with him and his wife, and his wife's sister, Mrs. Hurlbut. These two ladies were half-breeds, but very finely educated and accomplished ladies. They spoke Ojibwa, French and English.

JOHN TANNER, THE INDIAN CAPTIVE.

Another noted character there, that I knew well, was John Tanner, the U. S. interpreter. Tanner was a white man, who was stolen by the Ojibwas. while a child, some time in the latter part of the last century, near Cincinnati, O., and taken to the Manitoba region, where he lived some years, becoming a thorough Indian in manners and ideas. At the time I knew him in 1830, or '32, he was about 45 years of age. He had totally forgotten his native tongue while in captivity, but afterwards regained its use, and was interpreter at the Indian agency when I saw him, at Sault Ste Marie. He had again adopted the dress and life of a white man, and had been married to a squaw, by whom he had three dirty, black half-breed children. His squaw had died, or else he got rid of her in some way, because while we were at Sault Ste Marie, he conceived the idea that if he could get a white wife, it would raise him in the social scale considerably. He therefore secured a new outfit of clothing, and went to Detroit, where, by false representations of his position and means at Sault Ste Marie, which he pretended were respectable, he succeeded in deceiving a young woman into marrying him. She was a poor girl, but respectable and well thought of, and a member of a Baptist church in Detroit. When she got back with him to Sault Ste Marie, and was taken to his hovel, and found his coarse and ignorant half-breed children there, she was terribly heart-broken. There was no help for it then, however, and she had to live with him, and make the best of it. We all pitied her sincerely and did all we could to help and encourage her. But her life for a few months must have been wretched. Tanner even abused her, as though she was a common squaw. In the meantime, a babe was born to her. She now saw that she must escape from him at all hazards. Some friends managed to get Tanner sent out of the way one day while a steamer was in port, bound for Detroit, and she slipped on the vessel, and thus got away. One of Tanner's sons became a Unitarian clergyman afterwards, but I have heard very disparaging statements regarding his unclerical conduct. While we were at Sault Ste Marie,

there was a doctor, Edwin James, an army surgeon at
Fort Brady, who was a fine scholar. He got Tanner to
tell him all his story of captivity among the Indians, and
all about their daily life and customs, and wrote quite
a book from his statements. Tanner finally came to a
wretched end, though that was after we had left there.
It was about 1846, I think, Mr. Schoolcraft, the Indian
agent, had a brother living there, whom Tanner believed
to have had improper relations with one of his daugh-
ters. Watching an opportunity, he shot Schoolcraft and
killed him. Tanner at once fled at full speed to the
forest, and was never seen again, alive. It was supposed
that he had gone back to the Red River Indians with
whom he had formerly lived. But years after that some
hunters found, in a swamp a few miles from the Sault,
the skeleton of a man with a gun lying by it. On ex-
amining the latter, it was recognized as Tanner's. It is
thought that the violence of his exertions in escaping
had burst a blood vessel.*

There were two or three good missionaries at Sault
Ste Marie, among whom was Rev. Jeremiah Porter, a
Presbyterian, who labored hard to convert the Indians

---

*The account of Schoolcraft's murder, and of Tanner's connection with it,
was the story believed for many years by every body at Sault Ste Marie.
But recently, (I am informed by Capt. Dwight H. Kelton, U. S. A.) that circumstances were developed during a few years past, which exonerate Tanner
from the crime of murder, and seem to prove that both Schoolcraft and Tanner
were victims of a third party. The really guilty party, says Capt. K., was an
officer of the U. S. army, stationed at Fort Brady, at that time (1846) who, for
motives which are explained by some old settlers who claim to know the facts,
felt it necessary to get rid of Schoolcraft, and throw the suspicion of the crime
on Tanner. He, therefore, (so they assert positively) killed Schoolcraft, and also
Tanner, burning the body of the latter in his house, so that all evidence of the
latter crime was, for a time at least, destroyed, and it was given out that Tanner
had fled, after killing Schoolcraft. The officer now believed guilty of this double
crime, subsequently went to Mexico, where he was cashiered for some offence,
and died a few years subsequently, in an interior town of New York.   W.

and held prayer meetings among them, but I do not believe that very many were changed much in that way. Some good was done in the temperance line, however. The Indians had been a wretchedly drunken set, but the missionaries persuaded many of them to sign the pledge. Even the squaws signed it. Some of the white men and soldiers were converted, however.

THE ADAMSES GO TO CHICAGO.

In 1833, Capt. Adams was transferred to Fort Dearborn, Chicago. We lived there a number of years, and were among the earliest settlers of what afterwards became the great city. I attend the annual re-unions of the old settlers now, with great pleasure. Hardly any one of the period of 1833, but myself, now remains. The wonderful changes I have seen, seem like a dream. Everything was primitive those days. We can hardly realize it now. I remember the trouble we had sometimes to light a fire. Capt. Adams would gather a handful of dry stuff, and fire a gun loaded with powder into it. Then we had to gather up the combustibles, and blow it, until it ignited into a flame. Others used a flint and steel, with tinder.

When the Florida war broke out in 1835, Capt. Adams was opposed to going. He had had enough of army life. So he left it, and we went to farming. Our subsequent life was quiet and happy. Capt. Adams lived to the age of 90 years, and enjoyed excellent health and activity up to that time. We have been blessed with ten children, and I have now some 25 or 30 grand-children, and several great-grand-children.

www.ingramcontent.com/pod-product-compliance
Lightning Source LLC
Chambersburg PA
CBHW022206020726
47496CB00008B/2901